THE WITCH'S CAT

AND THE

BROOMSTICK BLUNDER

To everyone who took The Witch's Cat into their
hearts after his first adventure. This one's for you.

Kirstie x

TELLTALE TOTS

Telltale Tots Ltd.
www.telltaletots.co.uk

First published in the United Kingdom by Telltale Tots Publishing 2021

ISBN: 978-1-914937-04-0

A CIP catalogue record for this book is available from the British Library.

Text and illustrations copyright © Kirstie Watson 2021

THE WITCH'S CAT

AND THE

BROOMSTICK BLUNDER

WRITTEN BY

Kirstie Watson

ILLUSTRATED BY

Magdalena Sawko

The Lovely Witch was always zipping here
and there on her broomstick.
The Witch's Cat gave it very little thought.
After all, riding a broomstick IS what
witches are supposed to do.

One night though, Cat watched closely as
The Lovely Witch prepared for her flight.

First, she put on her hat and cloak.

Next, she sprinkled the broom with magic witching dust.

Then, she jumped aboard and said the magic words,
"One, two, three, four, five. Make this broomstick come alive!"

The broomstick went BANG! FIZZZZ! POP! and started to fly. Then the witch said, "Six, seven, eight, nine, ten. Broomstick go back down again!" and it landed back on the ground.

"I almost forgot! Cat, no mischief whilst I'm gone and absolutely NO magic!" she warned, before zooming off into the night.

Cat watched in awe, longing to fly a broomstick just like The Lovely Witch.

"How hard could it possibly be?" he said, digging
out a dusty old broomstick.
If it worked, he'd be able to go everywhere with
the witch – like a proper witch's cat.

"Hmmm, if only there was a book to help me learn," he thought. "Never mind, I'll work it out for myself."

He tried to remember what The Lovely Witch did first. Then it came to him...

"Ah ha! First, she put on her hat and cloak!"
So, he quickly put on a big witch's hat and a
long cloak, and hopped onto the broom.

He held on tightly as the broomstick started to shudder.

SPLUTTER, PUFF, PARRRPFFFF!

But then it just stopped. It hadn't worked.
"What else did The Lovely Witch do?" he wondered.

"I know! She probably thinks magical thoughts.
Well, that's easy, I'm an expert at magic."

So he thought and thought and THOUGHT as hard as
he could. But it didn't work.

"I'm sure The Lovely Witch said something...
'Cat, absolutely NO magic!'

No that's not it... it was something else. Was it...

'One, two, three, four, five.

Make this broomstick come alive!?'"

BAAAAANG! FIZZZZ! POP!

It worked. The broomstick burst into life.

Cat held on tightly as it whipped around the room.

Just when he thought it might never stop, his cloak caught on something, sending him crashing down to the ground.

"I can't believe it!" he said, dusting himself off.
"It actually **WORKED!** I just need a bit more practice!"

But this time, as he uttered the magic words,
"One, two, three, four, five.
Make this broomstick come alive!"
...absolutely NOTHING happened.

"Hmmm. What now?" he said, trying to think what The Lovely Witch would do. "Ah ha! Perhaps it needs some more witching dust!"

"THAT'S IT!" he said, giving the broomstick an extra good sprinkling of magic witching dust.

The broomstick instantly started to SHUDDER and SHAKE, then it started to SPARKLE and FIZZ.

"This is it!" Cat shouted excitedly. Then he uttered the magic words once again...

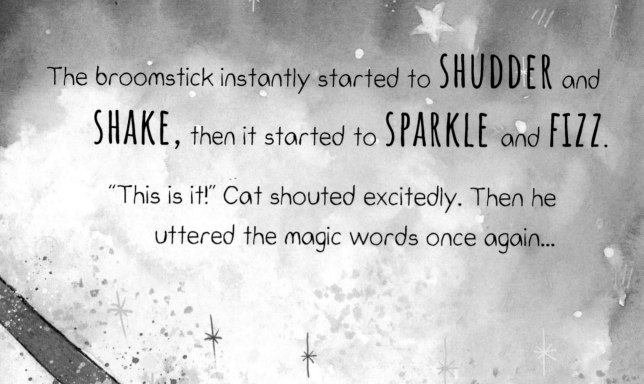

"One, two, three, four, five. Make this broomstick come alive!"

BAAAAANG! FIZZZZ! POP!

It worked! He clung on tightly as the broom blasted through the ceiling and out into the night's sky.
"DOWN! I WANT TO GO DOWN!" he yelled.

He was sure that there were some magic words
for this, but he just couldn't remember them now.

"DOWN, BROOMSTICK, DOWN!" he tried again.
But the broomstick had other ideas...

It flew up, down,
    loop-the-loop, over
the village then across...
    ...cities...

...forests...

...oceans...

...deserts...

...icebergs...

...jungles.

It went all around the world and back again.

He arrived home just as the broom began
to make some strange noises.

SPLUTTER, PUFF, PARRRPFFFF!

"Phew. That was... amazing! If not utterly TERRIFYING,"
said Cat as he sneaked back inside, only to be met by...

...A very unhappy witch.

"CAT! Look at all this mess!? Wait, you haven't been riding that broomstick have you?" she asked.

"Well, yes. I wanted to learn so I could come with you," he explained.

"That's lovely, Cat, but with magic, you must ALWAYS read the small print," said the witch picking up the empty jar.

The Lovely Witch forgave him (eventually), but he was NEVER allowed to ride a broomstick EVER again – which suited him just fine.

He'd already decided what he wanted to play with next.

I HOPE YOU'VE ENJOYED THIS STORY!

Did you know that reader reviews are like MAGIC for an author like me? They help bring attention to the book, and help others decide if they'd enjoy it too.

So, if you like this book, please consider...

1. Telling your FRIENDS about it.

2. Telling ME! I'd love to hear from you.

Send me a message via: kirstiewatsonauthor.co.uk

3. Leaving a REVIEW on Amazon or Goodreads.

Kirstie x

GRAB A FREE WITCH'S CAT ACTIVITY PACK!

Download from: kirstiewatsonauthor.co.uk/resources

FIND OUT MORE ABOUT KIRSTIE AND HER BOOKS:

f facebook.com/kirstiewatsonauthor

instagram.com/kirstie_watson_author

Made in the USA
Las Vegas, NV
11 October 2023

78936899R00024